T0197649

Gracie's Night Out

Bobbi Schlosser
Author and Illustrator

© Copyright 2021 *Bobbi Schlosser*.

All rights reserved. No part of this publication may be reproduced, stored in a retrieval system, or transmitted, in any form or by any means, electronic, mechanical, photocopying, recording, or otherwise, without the written prior permission of the author.

Order this book online at www.trafford.com or email orders@trafford.com

Most Trafford titles are also available at major online book retailers.

 www.trafford.com

North America & international
toll-free: 844 688 6899 (USA & Canada)
fax: 812 355 4082

Our mission is to efficiently provide the world's finest, most comprehensive book publishing service, enabling every author to experience success. To find out how to publish your book, your way, and have it available worldwide, visit us online at www.trafford.com

Because of the dynamic nature of the Internet, any web addresses or links contained in this book may have changed since publication and may no longer be valid. The views expressed in this work are solely those of the author and do not necessarily reflect the views of the publisher, and the publisher hereby disclaims any responsibility for them.

Any people depicted in stock imagery provided by Getty Images are models, and such images are being used for illustrative purposes only.
Certain stock imagery © Getty Images.

ISBN: 978-1-6987-0575-0 (sc)
ISBN: 978-1-6987-0574-3 (e)

Library of Congress Control Number: 2021902671

Print information available on the last page.

Trafford rev. 03/23/2021

This book is dedicated to my precious Great Grandchildren who continue to bless my life.

Carter David
Neveah Amor
Ellianna Reign
Journey Louise

Every day is a chance to listen and learn.

The Momma opened the door and suddenly, Gracie slipped out.

"Gracie, you get back here!" the Momma called. Gracie just ignored her and kept on going.

Gracie had never been outside before and wanted to see what it was all about. It was beginning to get dark but she wasn't afraid.

The moon was peeking through the clouds and Gracie thought it would be a great night to explore.

She came to a clearing and saw an animal that she had never seen before. He said "Hi, my name is Skunk. I think that we are related because when I was little, they called me a "Kit". Gracie said, "I don't think we are from the same family and besides that, you kind of smell!"

Skunk put his nose in the air and said "Well fine, I don't want to be your friend any way!" and walked away.

Gracie kept walking and there was an animal bent over eating some corn on the ground.

"Hello, what's your name?" said Gracie. The animal said "Oh, you scared me! I'm Deer. "Gracie said, "That's a nice name. My Momma calls me "Dear" sometimes too". "Your not a Deer", said the animal. "Well, you don't have to be rude", said Gracie and she walked on.

As Gracie was walking beside the road, there was a raccoon nearby. He said," Hey, what are you doing out here tonight?" Gracie said, "I'm just looking around".

The raccoon said, "Well, let's go out in the road and play!" Gracie said, "Oh, myMomma told me to never go near the road! "Oh, come on, don't be a scaredy cat!" said the raccoon. "No thanks" Gracie said and went on her way.

The moon went behind the clouds and it was hard for Gracie to see. Suddenly she stepped on something and it made a loud squeak. She looked down and saw a small animal under her foot. "Please don't eat me!" said the animal.

"I'm not going to eat you! Why would I do that?" said Gracie. "Because that's what cats do! They eat mice!" said the mouse.

"Well, I don't. I eat cat food that my Momma gives me," said Gracie.

"Then why are you out here in the dark and not in your nice warm house?" mouse said. "Because I wanted to see what the other animals were doing". Gracie said.

The mouse said "Well, I can tell you that we don't have a Momma to fix us a nice dinner" and he scurried off.

Gracie kept walking and soon came upon a squirrel gathering nuts.

"What are you doing?" asked Gracie. "I'm getting my food together for winter, are you hungry?" said the squirrel. "Yes, I am" Gracie said.

"Here, help yourself to some acorns", squirrel said. "No thank you, do you have any cat food?" said Gracie.

"Now why would a squirrel have cat food? You better go home," he said and began to climb the tree.

By this time, Gracie wanted to find her way home but she had forgotten which way she had come.

She saw a rabbit and asked him what he was eating. He said, "I'm eating grass and weeds". Gracie said, "Is that all you have to eat?" The rabbit said, "Yes, there is plenty! Help yourself, if you would like some". Gracie just shook her head and said

"No, thank you" and walked on down the path in the woods.

Gracie kept walking in the dark and by this time she was getting very hungry. She saw a strange looking animal and said," Who are you?"

The animal said, "I'm Opossum". Gracie noticed that he was eating supper like the other animals and asked him what he was eating. The Opossum said, "I'm eating garbage and there's not enough for you!" Gracie said, "Yuck!" and walked away.

"It's getting darker and I'm getting very hungry and tired", Gracie said out loud.

Suddenly, she heard a voice say, "You better get used to it if you're going to stay out here". She turned and saw another cat. "Are you exploring too?" Gracie said.

"No, I live out here", said the stray cat. "You mean you don't have a house to live in or a Momma to fix your dinner?" said Gracie.

In a sad voice the other cat said," No, I'm not that lucky" and laid down on his bed of leaves.

As Gracie began to walk away, she heard a very loud, "WHOO are you?"

She looked up and saw an owl sitting on a tree branch. She said, "I'm Gracie and I'm lost and hungry and I want to go home!"

The owl said," Why didn't you listen to your Momma when she told you not to run away?" Gracie said, "I don't know, but I don't like it out here!"

The owl said, "Alright, I'm going to show you the way home, but from now on you listen to your Momma!" He flew slowly ahead so Gracie could follow him out of the woods.

Gracie walked and walked and finally Owl said, "Here is your house Gracie and remember what I said about listening to your Momma ", and he flew off.

Gracie stood outside the house and meowed loudly. The Momma opened the door and picked Gracie up. As she hugged her, the Momma said, "Oh, Gracie I was so worried about you!"

Gracie snuggled up tightly and said, "Oh, Momma, I don't want to ever run away again!"

The End

Bobbi is the head of the Arts and Crafts Department at a center for those with special needs. She feels blessed to be able to use her gift of Art with them.

"Gracie's Night Out", is the second book that she has written and illustrated about cats that she has taken in. The first book is titled "Pilgrim" and is a true story about a cat that she found along the road with a can stuck on his head, two days before Thanksgiving.

Gracie was adopted from the local Humane Society in her area.

A message from Gracie

Thank you to all of the people that love,
protect, and take care of the animals
everywhere. Your fur friend, Gracie

Printed in the United States
by Baker & Taylor Publisher Services